No Longer Afraid

We love you, Liz Heaney,
our editor and friend.

NO LONGER AFRAID
© 1992 by A Corner of the Heart

Published by Multnomah Press Books
P.O. Box 1720
Sisters, Oregon 97759

Printed in the United States of America.

Questar Publishers, Inc.
Post Office Box 1720
Sisters, Oregon 97759

No Longer Afraid

LIVING WITH CANCER

BY DORIS SANFORD
ILLUSTRATIONS BY GRACI EVANS

MULTNOMAH PRESS

Jaime was tired. Too tired to play. Too tired to eat. She sensed that something was wrong. The lump on her neck was obviously worrying her parents. They took her to visit one doctor after another, each one poking her and asking questions. They always said, "Let's wait and see." Wait and see *what?* No one ever explained *that* part.

By December she was not just feeling tired, she was also feeling sick. The doctor called the lump on her neck a "growth." He wanted Jaime to have a biopsy, which he would send to a special laboratory near Jaime's grandparents' home in another state. One night a few weeks before Christmas Jaime overheard her dad say he wanted to be near this large research hospital "in case the news about the biopsy was 'bad.' "

During the long drive to her grandparents, Jaime curled up in the large, soft blanket in the back of the station wagon. It was snowing hard as she looked out of the window but she felt warm and cozy and secure. She knew that whatever was wrong, her parents would make it all right again.

They arrived on Christmas Eve. The aunts and uncles and cousins were already there. That afternoon her mom and dad went into a bedroom and phoned the research hospital. When they came out, Jaime could see by their faces that the news wasn't good. She quickly said, "If it's bad, don't tell me until after Christmas." They nodded.

Christmas morning! The yummy smells from Grandma's kitchen slipped under the door of Jaime and her cousins' room. For a few minutes she forgot how sick she felt. She knew the routine. Eat breakfast first. *Slowly* chew every bite. Wait to be excused by Grandpa. Jaime was sure the grown-ups could have eaten faster. Grandpa pretended they had all day to eat. He loved teasing the children.

"Daddy, am I gonna die?" A long pause.

"Honey, you're going to be just fine," and then his voice changed, "Remember, no sad talk on Christmas Day," and that was the end of the discussion.

After breakfast they would walk in the woods. Every other year she had loved the walk, but today she was too tired and could only take a few steps now and then. Her dad carried her on his shoulders. When they were alone behind the others, Jaime leaned down and whispered in his ear, "Daddy, is there a Taco Bell in heaven?" No answer.

The rest of the day was just as it had always been with presents, singing, tying Christmas ribbons on the dog's collar, and the wonderful smell of fresh-baked pies.

The next morning Mom and Dad said they needed to talk to her. Jaime knew bad news was coming. "You have cancer, Jaime. We have to take you to the hospital so they can give you a special medicine called chemotherapy." Jaime screamed, ran to the couch, and cried and yelled, "I'm going to die, aren't I?"

"No, Jaime, we're going to the hospital so they can *help* you. We need to leave right away."

As the car pulled out of the driveway, Jaime looked back and saw her sisters. Jackie was staring blankly and Summer was crying. All of the cousins were waving.

As they drove away, Jaime was full of questions. "What is cancer?"

"It's cells that have become different."

"Huh?"

"It's like having weeds in a garden."

"Huh?"

"It's like Pac-Man when the bad cells gobble up the good ones. It's sort of like a war, Jaime."

"Oh. Did it happen because I was bad?"

"No, honey. It just happened. Nothing you did caused this cancer."

"What will happen to me at the hospital? No more shots, Mom, please don't let them stick me, please . . ."

When they arrived at the large hospital, the nurse gave Jaime a bracelet with her name on it.

She had settled into her room when a nurse came in. She smiled first, and then said, "We need to start an IV." No amount of crying or screaming would stop the nurse. Fifteen minutes later Jaime was exhausted, but the IV had started. The nurse told her the IV was needed for the medicine.

The next morning Jaime overheard the doctors talking in the hall. "The cancer is on her lungs, ribs, spine, pelvis, and legs." It was the first time Jaime understood just how sick she was.

The day after she started taking the medication, the growth on her neck was half the size it had been. The next day it was gone.

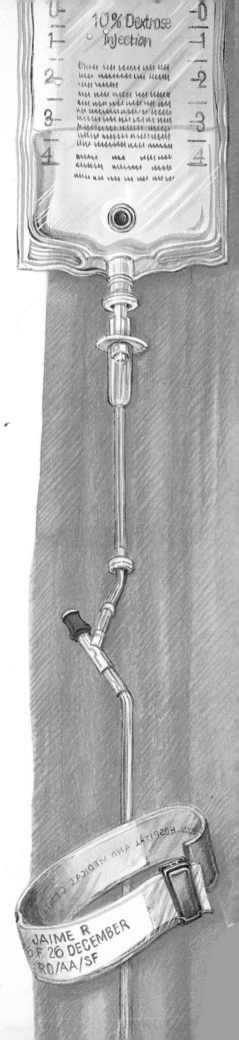

The following week Jaime had many blood tests. That was the worst part. Every time adults came into the room Jaime looked to see if they had the blood test kit. She didn't want to smile at someone who was going to hurt her! Whenever Jaime's temperature rose to one degree above normal, the nurses would draw her blood.

Jaime's eyebrows and eyelashes fell out because of the chemotherapy. Her mom finally cut Jaime's hair because it was coming out in handfuls. In the children's cancer unit at the hospital she would have looked strange *with* hair!

Mom slept beside her every night at the hospital. Jaime was glad about that. She was never alone. Each night when the lights were out, her mom held her hand and sang the lullaby:

> So, slumber, sweet angel
> And don't fear the night
> God will be watching and holding you tight.
> May each wish that you dream
> Be a star shining bright
> With Mommy beside you 'til
>   morning's first light.[1]

1. Steve Siler, "Don't Fear the Night," (Fifty States Music, 1991). Used by permission.

12

Jaime was in the hospital for ten days. The doctors told her that to prevent the cancer from growing again, she would have to continue chemotherapy for two years.

Jaime couldn't go back to her regular classroom because she might catch an infection. She also needed a lot of rest during the day. The chemo made her throw up. She was sure the kids at school would prefer that she stay home until she was finished with *that!* Her mother decided to home-school her.

One very important trip was wig-shopping day. Her first wig was a short, curly one, an "Orphan Annie look-alike."

On her tenth birthday, Jaime went for a drive. When she returned home her mother suggested she go to her room. She pulled off her hot, scratchy wig on the way upstairs. When she opened the door there were thirteen girls jumping and yelling, "Happy Birthday!"

"Wow, I've never seen you without hair before," one girl said. Jaime wasn't embarrassed because they were all her friends. After they all tried on her wig, they decided it looked best on Jaime.

After that the bald jokes began. "Hey, Jaime, I like your chemo cut." "Jaime, is your hair coming or going?" Jaime learned to respond with humor, "My father is Kojak," or, "I just joined the marines."

Whenever she was riding in the car, she waited until another car was next to them and then she lifted her wig. It was so much fun to watch the faces of the children! At a stoplight once she rolled down the window and hollered, "See what will happen to you if you don't eat your vegetables?"

When her friends asked her if she liked her wig, she said, "Get real! Who wants to look like Eva Gabor when you're ten years old?"

It was fun to laugh. Jaime needed time out from the sadness of her illness. Her mother had saved her hair for the birds to use in making nests. She had seen several nests with soft blonde curls.

In the fall she was back at the private school she had attended since first grade. It was good to be with her friends again. She was still taking chemo, still wearing the wig, but life felt normal.

On Halloween she attended a harvest party with her family and that night she became ill. She couldn't catch her breath, her heart pounded when she walked, and she was too tired to play. She was afraid it was the cancer again. It wasn't. The doctor said her heart was having a bad reaction to the chemo and she would have to stop taking the drugs to treat her cancer. He looked sad when he said it.

She almost forgot about being sick. But then in January when she went back for her doctor's appointment he found a new lump. *No! No! No! It can't be happening!*

Jaime thought the doctor must have made a mistake. He said, "No mistake, Jaime. You will have to go back to the hospital."

Having a relapse is like going to Disneyland and finding it closed. Maybe worse than that. Her parents took her to a special clinic in another state so she could get special foods and vitamins for two weeks. They said it might help. For sure it wouldn't hurt. After they left the clinic they headed back home. She would enter the hospital tomorrow.

She knew the doctors would start an IV. They did. It was going to be put in her chest so the chemo would go in near her heart. They would give her new drugs that wouldn't hurt her heart this time.

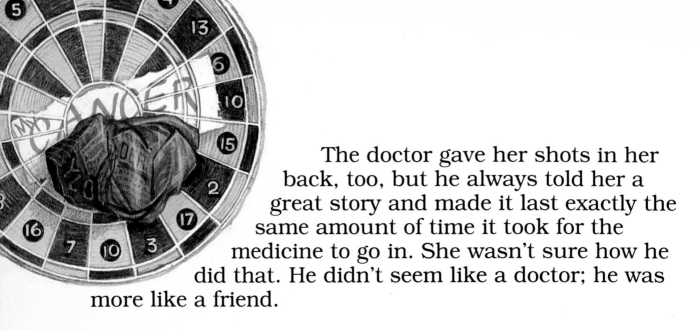

The doctor gave her shots in her back, too, but he always told her a great story and made it last exactly the same amount of time it took for the medicine to go in. She wasn't sure how he did that. He didn't seem like a doctor; he was more like a friend.

It was good that she had friends at the hospital because many of her school friends were too busy to visit her and she was lonely. Once her teacher came when Jaime was drawing pictures. She said, "Are you going to be an artist when you grow up?" Jaime said, "I *am* an artist."

Sometimes she ate in her room and sometimes in the playroom. It was nice to have a choice about something. She had taught herself to say, "I can handle this" before receiving shots. She had grown so much since she first became sick.

She asked lots of questions. "Why did I get cancer?" "What will happen next?" "Are you sure that the medicine will help me?" They couldn't answer *any* of the important questions. They did promise to tell her the truth about anything that would hurt. She was glad about that. She wasn't into surprises!

When she went to the playroom, the child-life therapist told her she could rip pages from a magazine and roll them up into little balls and throw them at a dart board lettered, MY CANCER. Once she drew her cancer cells on a pillowcase and the therapist let her punch it. It felt good. No one told her how to feel in the playroom. Feelings just were. They weren't good or bad.

Finally, after two weeks, she could leave the hospital. When the staff came to say good-bye Jaime said, "Thank you, and I hope I never see you again." They smiled and said, "You're welcome, and we hope we don't see you here again, either." They all laughed.

That night at home she thought about the friends she had made at the hospital, especially the ones who had died. Going to sleep was hard because she kept thinking about the memories.

Jaime loved the nights that her best friends, Teresa and April, slept over. One of their favorite games was asking, "If you could have anything in the world, what would it be?" Teresa and April had many choices, but Jaime always said the same thing. She wanted to be a horse trainer when she grew up and she wanted a Morgan horse of her own. Her family owned a horse and Jaime loved it, but there was something special about a Morgan. She dreamed about Morgans, read about them, collected pictures of them, and wrote stories about Morgans.

So when the lady from Make a Wish Foundation, a national organization that grants wishes to children with life-threatening illnesses, came to the door and told her that they would like to make her dream come true, Jaime could hardly believe it. She kept pinching herself. Really? Honest and truly, she would own a Morgan? And, not only that; she would also be the assistant judge at the next Far West Regional Morgan Horse Association show. She couldn't sleep or eat. She had to study the book about how to judge Morgans.

The show day finally came. She wanted to go to the arena early. Two hours early. Her family laughed. If Jaime had her way, they all would have slept in sleeping bags on the bleachers the night before!

The crowd gathered and the music came over the loudspeakers.

Jaime entered in a horse-drawn carriage while the music played, "When You Wish upon a Star." She was so happy, she cried.

When she arrived at the judges' row, one of the judges smiled and said, "I think your happiness is leaking out of your eyes." It was!

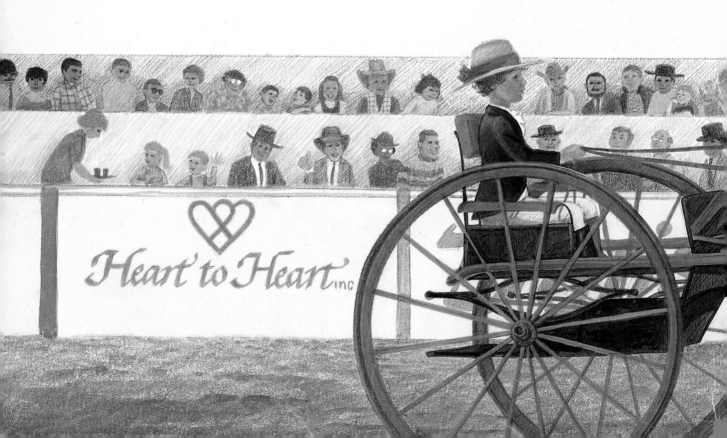

Heart to Heart inc

The horses were paraded by. She knew what to look for and she marked her numbers on the score card. It was to be the second most exciting day of her life. The *most* exciting day would be the day her own Morgan arrived. She didn't know when she would receive her horse, but the search had begun with ads in national horse magazines.

Finally it happened. The phone call came. They had found the perfect horse for Jaime. The horse was in another state and would be shipped soon. The Make a Wish Foundation would present the horse at the state fair in September. The horse's name was Jetrae Love. Jaime's middle name was also Rae. They belonged together. She could be called Jetta, for short.

The presentation was at noon. TV cameras were everywhere. Relatives and hundreds of people stood by to watch the magical moment. The state fair officials presented Jaime with a basket of roses and then Jetta was brought in. Her hooves were painted and she wore a wreath of glitter and red roses. The crowd held their breath and all eyes were on Jaime. It was love at first sight. When Jaime could talk, she patted Jetta and said, "You're everything I always wanted." Now *everyone* was crying!

The Morgan Horse Association would provide a trainer for Jetta and teach Jaime how to handle her. Jake had been training horses for a long time. Jetta was in good hands. Jetta wouldn't be able to get away with anything with Jake.

Jaime and Jetta would spend lots of time together in the next months and when they were finished, Jetta would know that Jaime was the boss.

Some days Jaime almost forgot she had cancer. She spent hours riding Jetta. She felt tall and free on Jetta's back. Occasionally someone would say something and she knew that she was never really far away from the disease. A lady at church had said, "You have to be strong; you don't have any choice." But Jaime knew she *did* have a choice. She could complain and stomp her feet, or she could enjoy each day as it came.

Each month Jaime went back to the cancer doctor for a blood test. She didn't know what would happen with the disease, but she knew that she was not the same person as when it began. Now she knew that whatever happened, she would be okay. She was no longer afraid of the dark.

Discussion Questions

1. How would you explain cancer to someone who had never heard about this disease?

2. Have you ever been in a hospital? Tell about it.

3. Like most kids, Jaime was afraid of having shots. What could she have done to help her with this fear?

4. The cancer treatment caused Jaime to lose her hair so she had to wear a wig. How did she handle this?

5. After Jaime received the chemotherapy she felt better. What do you think she thought and felt when she found a *new* lump?

6. What could you do to help a friend who is in the hospital?

7. Jaime dreamed of owning a Morgan horse. What dreams do you have?